Benjamin's Gift

Benjamin's Gift

Charles R. Callaway

ILLUSTRATED BY GLOY WRIDE
COVER ILLUSTRATION BY RICHARD HOLDAWAY

D

Distribution:
Origin Book Sales
6200 S. Stratler St.
Murray, UT 84107
1-888-467-4446

To my loving wife Linda
and children:
Dallas, Dustin, Derrick, Jaclyn,
Sterling, Christian.

olding tight to the sides of a Roman helmet, Benjamin tried desperately to put it on before Lancus, his brother, came through the door. Pulling hard, he finally placed the helmet firmly on his head. For an instant, a feeling of grandeur and power stirred him. How great he would look as a Roman soldier!

Then, as always, the realization of the impossibility of such an accomplishment brought him face to face with his usual "if only". If only there was a chance to prove to himself and the other boys his age that he could do the same things they were able to do: climb trees, run races, and most of all, play kickball, the main sport in Judea.

Hot humid waves of blistering heat washed over the young boys as they played kickball outside in the town courtyard. Dodging from side to side so as not to be hit, the boys enjoyed their fun as Benjamin looked on from inside. Big tears filled his eyes as he remembered the many times Samuel and Jason had rejected him. How he longed to play in the sunshine, to run, to jump, to laugh — to do all the things other boys could do.

Lancus came into the room and moved quickly to the window where his little brother was sitting. "What's the helmet on for? You're no soldier! Herod would kill anyone who tried to mock his great army!"

"I'm not mocking it," said Benjamin. "I just wanted to try it on."

"Anyone without legs is a mockery to his great strength. Be sure the helmet is polished up by morning. I leave for Canatha early. It will be a short war. I'll be back within three months. It is only a border disturbance."

Benjamin's father and mother had died in an accident five years earlier while on a trip to Jericho. Lancus was left with the responsibility of rearing his little brother, Benjamin,who had been born with only two short stumps where his legs should have been.

Life during the last five years had been hard for both of the brothers, especially for Benjamin whose handicap limited his friendships as well as his activities. During these lonely days, Benjamin sat quietly at the window of his home and carved small animals from scraps of wood which he sold later by the street.

As for Lancus, his hopes and desires were centered on gaining power and authority. King Herod had a strong influence on the minds of the young men as they trained for his great army. Lancus saw his chance to gain his desired place of power and importance as part of Herod's army.

Wiping the tears from his eyes, Benjamin continued to look out the window as Lancus hurried out the door. "I'm not a mockery. I mean no harm to anyone."

lightly changing its course of direction, the cool breeze descended out of the hills surrounding Jerusalem as Benjamin felt of its arrival. The hurt in his heart eased as he looked up into the stars catching a glimpse of the vastness of God's creations. The peace and quiet of this secluded place had been his refuge from the curious stares of people and the cutting pain of being ignored by those who could have given him companionship.

For three years now he had been going to Jacob's olive orchard. Jacob had taken him there once out of friendship for Benjamin's dead parents. Seeing Benjamin's speechless joy after a day alone outdoors, Jacob made a point of taking him out after each market day and bringing him back in the evening. Lancus was relieved and Benjamin was passionately grateful.

The gentle breeze stirring the olive branches, the glorious blue of the sky dotted with clouds of white and the quiet movements of the little animals living there brought a peaceful hope and renewed strength to the heart of Benjamin. Popping up out of its hole, a brown furry ground squirrel came near Benjamin. He reached his arms toward it in welcome. The squirrel came no closer, but neither did it run away. It sat in front of Benjamin chewing it's food fast and rhythmically. The little animals here in Jacob's orchard had a special place in Benjamin's heart. They gave him no critical stares and accepted him as their friend, for he made no movements or noise that would disturb their peaceful lives.

Often coming to his secluded spot helped him feel the joy and happiness which he rarely felt in Jerusalem. Dreams of being a hero captured the center of his attention. Ever since Benjamin's parents had died, he was starved for love and affection which he had enjoyed so many years before. Benjamin would reminisce about the experiences he had enjoyed with his parents. He remembered his father telling him to be kind to everyone, no matter what they did to him. Now as he grew older, he often wondered if his father knew how hard it would be to follow his teachings; and yet as he meditated, he knew this was the only way he could win the hearts of people. He could not be a Roman soldier, nor could he have the influence of a wealthy merchant. His only tool would be the power of love. He remembered his mother's great concern for him as she once said, "Benjamin, remember these four things: Know yourself, know who you are. Control yourself, hurt no one. Give of yourself to help others. Find ways to help everyone you meet. You may not be able to lift great physical burdens for others, but you can lift the heavy burdens of their hearts which will bring happiness to their souls. The level of your service will be to the level of your happiness."

These teachings had found root in Benjamin's heart and

often he would lie awake at night thinking of ways he could help others to be happy. However, no one seemed to want his help. "What?" he wondered sadly, "could a cripple do anyway?" Yet, lying in the grass Benjamin could hear the bees humming through the air which lifted his spirits. He felt a nearness to God, who was more powerful than all the Roman army. Looking down upon Jerusalem from the side of the hill gave him an inspiration that was overwhelming. Lights were shimmering afar off in the humid summer night as if millions of fire flies were held under a large glass dome. Deep in his heart he felt the truth of the prophets' story that a savior would come and bring peace and love into the world.

fter making a few short stabs with his sword, Lancus stepped back from the stuffed dummy to view his kill. "Bravo! Bravo!" cried the young warriors. Lancus looked up to acknowledge his peers and saw King Herod clapping vigorously, complimenting the style of the young soldier. Lancus smiled broadly, then raising his sword, shouted, "Hail King Herod." Other warriors gathered around Lancus and raising their swords in unison, cried out, "Hail, King Herod!"

There was great excitement in the training courtyard as Herod's army prepared for battle. A day earlier Lancus had been appointed Herod's command leader. Being King Herod's army

leader had been a dream Lancus had cherished since boyhood.

During the last few years, the commandments taught to Lancus by his parents had become less important to him, while the glory of achievement in the army had become more desirable and more rewarding. Obeying the teachings of the prophets gave no promise of power and recognition he so much desired. Obedience to Herod had already rewarded him with the attention he had never before been given. The memory of the teachings of his parents became dim, pride filled his heart and basking in his new found glory he gave Herod his complete loyalty and obedience.

By early afternoon, the clanging of armor echoed through the Kedron Valley as Herod's army marched toward their destination. Coming closer to the opening of the valley, Lancus and his army could see the low level plains which led to the mountains of Sychar.

"Halt!"

Thousands of feet stopped immediately upon hearing the command of their leader. Lancus knelt down by the brook and filled his camel skin water bag. The soldiers followed in unison in preparation for their long march across the hot sandy desert.

Lancus raised to his feet. The ravens circling above seemed like an omen of success for him. As their strong wings carried them over all obstacles, his strong arm would wield his flashing sword over his enemies.

illing his basket with small wooden carvings, Benjamin prepared to take his place on the street in front of his house in hopes of selling many. He glanced around to make sure he hadn't missed any. Taking the basket he slowly made his way, half crawling, half shuffling out the door and down the steps to the roadside.

Holding up a carving he would often say, "Would you like to buy a gift for someone you love?" Most people went on their hurried way and paid no attention to his plea. Now and then, however, some stopped, maybe out of pity or maybe because they appreciated Benjamin's fine work.

Benjamin had been in the street for some time when a large man stopped and said, "Hello, young man. What are you selling?"

Benjamin smiled hopefully. "Wooden horses, doves, sheep or I can carve you anything you want!"

"You're quite the merchant, aren't you?"

"I hope so," Benjamin answered.

The man put his hand into his pouch. Benjamin looked up hopefully. The man pulled his hand from his pouch and stooped to put the coins into Benjamin's hand. There was money for three carvings. Benjamin gave a surprised and tearful, "Thank you! Thank you!"

The following day, Benjamin was on the street selling

again. The day always began with high hopes; but as the hours passed and there were no sales, weariness and discouragement overcame Benjamin. It was time to go home to pray and hope for a better tomorrow.

Benjamin's straw bed supported by low wooden blocks invited him to rest and he lay wearily down. He wondered if he would ever sell enough carvings to pay Jacob for the wooden legs he was making for him. Jacob insisted that he did not want to be paid. He wanted to make the legs because he loved Benjamin. Yet, Benjamin could not forget Jacob's large family and all their needs. He knew that Jacob's carpentry work was their only means of support. He must carve more and sell more.

Years earlier Jacob and Benjamin's father had worked together. They had become very close and much was to be said of their enduring friendship. After the death of Benjamin's father, Jacob felt a keen desire to look after Benjamin. His desire was heightened even more because of Lancus' absence.

Benjamin's thoughts then turned to the joy he would experience with his new legs. The anticipation was almost too great. No longer would he sit by the road looking at hurried feet passing by — rarely to see someones face unless they chose to stop.

When he received his new legs he would stand tall, look into their faces and see their smiles. His brightened countenance would let them know he was a friend with something beautiful to sell.

"I could do so much more for others if I only had legs,"

Benjamin thought.

Then turning to bow his head he prayed, "Oh please God, help me sell enough carvings to pay for the wooden legs. I need them so much."

At night he pleaded with words. During the day his heart sent a prayer above. Weariness overcame him and Benjamin slept.

ays of sunshine broke through the trees outside Benjamin's house. Little doves lined most of the branches of the sycamore trees and their cooing was a cheerful beginning for Benjamin's new day. Already vendors were at work in the streets.

Soon Benjamin was at his usual selling place, cheerfully explaining to a customer what kind of wood the little lamb had been carved from.

Selling day after day, the days turned into weeks and the weeks into months as he saved for the wooden legs which he hoped would make such a difference in his life. In his dreams he could play with the boys. He would have friends.

He saw himself walking down the streets of Jerusalem seeing all the things he had only heard about. Buildings which he had only seen from a distance would then be at his fingertips.

The challenges and the possibilities which the new legs

would bring into his life filled him with excitement, and now his prayer was one of gratitude for this blessing yet to come.

Benjamin's selling day was over once more and he was home. It had been a good day. He was anxiously waiting for a knock on his door, for Jacob was to bring his new wooden legs. Thinking about them gave Benjamin a nervous stomach. He felt like he had a thousand butterflies flying around inside of him. He tried to think about his little animal friends in Jacob's olive orchard, but his thoughts always seemed to come back to his new wooden legs. Just then the latch on the door rattled, followed by a loud knock. Startled, Benjamin quickly came back to reality and with greater anticipation and excitement made his way to the door on his short stumps. Reaching high he lifted the door latch and there stood Jacob holding the wooden legs. Benjamin looked at them in surprise. The fine polished wood told him that it had come from as far north as Jerusalem, maybe even Lebanon. He moved his hands slowly across the hard surface. It could withstand the bumps and falls that would come as he learned to walk. The round base would help him balance.

"Oh Jacob, come in. Do you think I'll be able to walk on them?"

"Oh yes, I'm sure you will. Here, why don't you sit down and I'll show you how to put them on."

Jacob strapped the padded wooden legs to the toughened stumps, then secured them to a belt around Benjamin's waist. Holding tight to Jacob's shoulder, Benjamin pulled himself up.

"Hang on to me," Jacob warned.

"I'll hold on to you. Don't worry. Oh, it's so different. I'm afraid."

Jacob moved to the other side of Benjamin to get a better position in helping him. Slowly, with Jacob's support Benjamin walked around the room. It wasn't as easy as he had pictured it would be. Jacob cautioned him, "It will be a long time before you'll get use to them. Be sure to keep the pads on your stumps so they won't get sore."

Benjamin accepted his new challenge and walked slowly — step by step — one leg in front of the other. As his confidence increased, he realized his blessing and tears filled his eyes. He put his arms around Jacob's neck.

"How could this be happening to me? God has answered my prayers. I am free to move about and go where I want to go."

Looking into Jacob's eyes, Benjamin gave a big sigh of relief.

"Thank you, Jacob. I hope God will bless you with the desires of your heart as he has mine."

Jacob with tearstained cheeks leaned closer to Benjamin and in a soft but choked voice said, "He already has! He already has!"

"Jacob, the legs are so wonderful. They mean so much to me. I haven't enough money saved now, but I will give more as I get it. I can never pay you enough for the joy you have given me."

Jacob put his arm around his young friend. "Benjamin," he said, "every minute I have worked on the legs I have been happy. Even while I waited for this special wood I was happy thinking about the joy that would come to you. Don't you know that the giver is happier than the receiver? Do you want to take away the joy that will live in my heart if I give the legs to you?"

Benjamin was thoughtful. He had not realized how

Jacob felt. He knew now what Jacob meant when he said that God had already blessed him with the desires of his heart.

After several days of practice on his new legs in and around his house, Benjamin decided to take his long desired walk into the busy streets of Jerusalem. It would give him a chance to see the many people, even to meet and talk to some he had never met before. As he made his way out onto the dusty street there were those who stopped to look at him as he made slow progress toward the buildings which he had only seen from a distance. Some people showed signs of wanting to help which had seldom been the case back on his home street. Others continued on their way not even noticing this great event which had come into Benjamin's life.

As he continued his journey, Benjamin's heart glowed with love for Jerusalem. It was his city now. He felt a part of it as he had never felt before. He loved the great buildings, the crowded streets and busy people. It was his home and he loved it all, for now he could be part of it's way of life.

The glow of that momentous day stayed with him even though succeeding days were not always as happy. The day he tried to play kickball with Samuel and Jason had almost been a disaster. The ball hit his legs and knocked him down more often than he could kick it.

With each passing day, Benjamin gained a new knowledge of people. Their reactions to Benjamin's appearance on his new legs and his ability to walk and even laugh, gave him the confidence which he needed. Benjamin frequently had mixed emotions about his new experiences. Occasionally he would laugh. Often he cried with frustration, but always he hoped and worked with determination to improve. He always ended the day with prayer and found comfort in knowing God would still bless him.

ancus had been gone for five months now and Benjamin was worried. There had been no word in Jerusalem about the army's progress after they had marched through the Kedron Valley on their way to the border.

This long absence helped Benjamin forget how Lancus had looked upon his handicap as a sign of weakness. Ashamed, Lancus always tried to avoid taking Benjamin into public with him. His absence even helped Benjamin forget the cutting remarks Lancus had made.

Now he remembered that Lancus had always kept food in their home and provided fresh straw for his bed. Before he had been appointed Herod's army commander, Lancus had been kind to Benjamin. Sometimes he even talked with him about their parents. Now after five months absence Benjamin missed Lancus. He longed for the feeling of security Lancus had given him. The love he had for his brother was deep and his heart ached for him.

Despite his worry, there were times when Benjamin's soul was filled with joy and satisfaction. During these past months Benjamin's sales had doubled, for now he could sell clear across town rather than on the single street to which he had been confined for so many years.

Jacob had been by often to see how Benjamin was getting along. He always expressed his happiness at knowing that he had been the one to put the joy of walking into Benjamin's life.

Benjamin's concern over the long absence of Lancus had plunged him into a deep depression. One night he asked Jacob, "Have you heard anything about Lancus?"

"No, I haven't."

Benjamin looked out the window then back toward Jacob. "There must be some reason for his being so long at war. If you hear anything please let me know."

Jacob had always been like a second father to Benjamin. Now as he rose to go he put his arm affectionately around Benjamin's shoulders. "I'll let you know, but remember, Benjamin, put your trust in the Lord and learn from each experience." Jacob turned, then left quietly.

For a few minutes, Benjamin sat thinking of Lancus. He didn't want to be alone. He longed for his brother. As he looked out his window, the quiet street seemed to offer some relief to his loneliness. He made his way down the steps to the street and by the light of the stars he followed the narrow pathway leading to the well at the north end of the city.

Since he had received his legs, this well had become one

of his favorite places. Here in the quiet of evening he could think and plan. He reached the well and pulled the wooden bucket to the surface. He drank of the cold water as he sat on the rock edge of the well.

All his thoughts were on Lancus. How he longed for him! If only Lancus would come home. He would be so happy to show him how he could walk. He would make Lancus proud of him. He knew they would appreciate each other. By the light of the stars, he followed the narrow pathway home to his bed and prayers.

enjamin was right to be worried about Lancus. Over six months earlier, Lancus had led his soldiers to the disputed border, arriving just as night fell. The enemy, the Canathian army, was encamped inside Judea. Lancus sent word along the long lines of his soldiers to halt the march, to make camp, and rest until morning.

Quickly, sentries took up positions and scouts moved stealthily about as they sought to find out the location and strength of the enemy army. Their reports went back to Lancus. In the pre-dawn darkness his direction, "Prepare for battle!," traveled quickly to his loyal and spirited young soldiers. Every soldier obeyed instantly, for they loved Lancus as a leader and had faith in him.

In the enemy camp, Philip, the Canathian leader gave the signal of readiness and every soldier responded. Philip thrust his sword into the rich soil, then, raising it high in the air gave the command, "Attack!"

Hundreds of Canathian soldiers moved quickly toward Herod's army expecting to take the camp by surprise. However, Lancus had proved his leadership and his men were prepared. The deadly battle began.

The morning air was filled with confusion of clashing swords, loud cries for victory, the moans of the wounded and the heavy breathing of the dying. Lancus was in the thick of the battle. Skillfully he blocked the slice of an enemy sword which would have buried itself into his body. Moving quickly, he sank his sword into the heart of his opponent. Parrying the thrusting, Lancus hewed his way across the battleground.

Suddenly he saw Contia, his own second-in-command was in mortal danger. While he dueled with an enemy soldier, another Canathian came from behind with his sword raised. Lancus hurled himself forward, dagger in hand, and killed Contia's assailant. The two leaders clasped hands, grinned and turned to continue the battle.

Lancus headed for higher ground to better his fighting position. Canathian soldiers moved to surround him but Lancus jabbed and chopped with mighty strength. Metal hitting metal the sword of Lancus continued to draw blood, wounding and killing enemy soldiers.

Other Canathians, seeing how the sword of Lancus was

cutting down their men, began to fall back. That part of Philip's fighting line began to waver and retreat.

Herod's men seeing the weakness in the enemy line felt a surge of added courage. Fighting became more frenzied. The enemy continued to retreat and soon Lancus could see that in a matter of moments they would break and run. Judea's border would be safe from her enemies. With victory emanate, Lancus raised his sword to the sky and triumphantly yelled, "Hail, King Herod! Hail, King Herod!"

Suddenly a spear blazed through the air and thudded, vibrating into Lancus' exposed back. He tottered, then fell, his life blood draining into the soil to mark the place where victory meant death.

Benjamin knew nothing of this tragedy as he learned that the war was over. From his window, Benjamin watched the rugged, tired soldiers as they marched up the cobblestone street. Even through his excitement, he noticed that these men did not look like the pompous and haughty warriors who had marched off to battle some months before. Eagerly, he scanned the ranks for a glimpse of Lancus, but no Lancus. Upon hearing a knock he reluctantly left his window to answer the door. There stood Contia, Herod's second-in-command. A sinking feeling swept over Benjamin. Why would Contia be here?

"May I come in?" he asked.

Benjamin opened the door wide and motioned him into the room. His terrified and questioning expression made Contia fumble for words.

"I wanted to stop and let you know that Lancus saved my life." Contia began.

"Where is he?" The words were almost a cry.

The invincible grandeur of Herod's second-in-command fell from him like a cloak. He stood before Benjamin an exhausted man near tears. Contia moved to Benjamin and put a gentle arm around his shoulder.

"He's dead." Contia's voice was husky.

"Dead! Dead!" Benjamin's words died in a choking sob.

"Yes," Contia continued, "he died just after raising his sword to King Herod. Lancus was a great leader, one of the greatest King Herod ever had. He told me about you and how he loved you. I hope I can do something to help you. I want to be your friend. After I report to King Herod, I will come back to see you." With a warm embrace that comforted Benjamin, Contia was gone.

Numbly, Benjamin followed Contia from the house and in stunned silence headed for Jacob's house. He needed Jacob.

Jacob was not at home but his wife told Benjamin she would send Jacob to him as soon as he came. The first terrible shock was over and Benjamin began to cry softly as he went home to wait for his friend.

As Jacob anchored two large beams on the house he was building, he overheard some women talking of Lancus' death. Gathering up his tools, he went straight for Benjamin's house. He knocked gently, then harder. No one answered. Quietly he opened the door and went in.

Benjamin, with tears dried on his face, was asleep on his bed. Jacob sat down waiting for him to awaken. When Benjamin stirred, Jacob said, "Benjamin, I wanted to talk to you. I'm so sorry about Lancus."

Benjamin sat up and Jacob put a comforting hand on his shoulder. His heart ached for this young boy who had become such a special part of his life. He hardly knew how to comfort him.

"Lancus was a good boy," Jacob began, "He was a great soldier. Like many people — in pursuit of their dreams — he forgot some of the other ways he could be great. I'm sure he felt he was doing what he thought was best."

Benjamin was comforted just having Jacob with him.

"Tell me again what your father told you to do, Benjamin," Jacob said.

"He said to be kind to everyone no matter what they did to me," Benjamin said, puzzled but obedient.

"Benjamin, you had a wise father. You know that in this busy land there is need for soldiers, carpenters, some to care for the house and the children, some to tend the sheep, some to run the city and some to carve wood and give beauty to others; but with all these jobs there should be love and concern for people. Thinking of others and working for their happiness is the way we find true happiness, Benjamin."

Jacob's reasoning caused Benjamin to think, to turn his thoughts from the loss of Lancus to how he might bring happiness to others. Jacob was relieved to see Benjamin's grief turn to interest.

"Come, Benjamin," he said, rising from the bed where they had been sitting. "Let's take a little walk over to my house. It's supper time. The family will be glad to have you and you know how the little boys love your stories about the little animals you see in the olive orchard.

Benjamin rose to go with Jacob and silently gave thanks for his close friend.

 lthough Benjamin continued to work at his carvings, his spirits were low and his own loneliness overshadowed his cheerful nature. Each day's work was routine and the purpose for life was gone. No longer was he looking for ways to help others. His own depression was bound to a spiritless routine.

On one particular evening, he gathered up the remaining carvings and started home.

"Wait," called a man, hesitating before him. "There is one called Jacob, a carpenter. Do you know where I can find him?"

"No," replied Benjamin. Then half aloud he added, "Is it my job to know where everybody is?"

Then turning, he continued his slow walk home. There was no need to hurry. At that lonely time of evening, Benjamin felt there was no need to do anything.

"No," repeated itself to him. Benjamin suddenly felt a

sickening disappointment in himself. He was no longer the boy who encouraged and helped people. He had joined those who had hurt him, those who had brought tears to him as a little boy and heartache as he had grown older.

He set his carvings down and hurried back as fast as he could to the corner where the man had approached him. There was no one in sight.

He said to himself sadly, "Stranger, I'll help you find Jacob. I know where he lives."

There was no one to hear him. He leaned against a building knowing that his attitude had destroyed his opportunity to help the man. He felt an emptiness. Something had gone out of him. That part of him which had been alive when he helped others was gone. He had destroyed a part of himself.

The hurt he had suffered in his life had made him mindful of others who needed help in any way. Now as he continued on his way home he questioned, "What has come over me? How could I be so cruel?"

Entering his house he found a large kettle of cooked wheat prepared by someone who had left no name. This added to his depressed feeling for he felt he was not worthy of this wonderful gift.

Removing his wooden legs, Benjamin knelt on his tired stumps by his bed and offered up his feelings to the God of heaven.

"I don't know why I've been so depressed. Please help me to be happy. I miss Lancus very much. Life isn't as happy as it used to be. Why am I so unhappy? I'm sorry I didn't help that man. Please forgive me! Please help me to give of myself to help others."

He felt complete sadness as he continued to plead for help to overcome his weaknesses and for mercy from Him who will forgive and show mercy.

Benjamin's parents had taught him well how to keep a close relationship with his Father in Heaven through prayer. That relationship had sustained him through many trials. Now he prayed for that sustaining power to come to his aid and comfort. Vowing that he would again put his life in tune through service, Benjamin fell asleep.

The next morning, as Benjamin was going to his favorite selling corner, he saw the man who had asked where Jacob lived the night before.

"Hello!" he greeted Benjamin.

"You are back! You came back! I know where Jacob lives."

Benjamin felt he had a second chance to undo the wrong of the night before.

"You do?" questioned the man.

"Yes, his house is the fourth one north of the cloth merchant's shop."

"Thank you, young man." The man hurried toward the shop.

Benjamin's heart quickened. Once again he felt joy. His depression was gone. The sun seemed brighter, hopes for a successful day mounted, and a smile with true warmth lit up his face. Gratitude filled Benjamin's soul. Silently, he gave thanks to the Father of us all for this experience which had brought peace to his heart, joy to his soul, and purpose to his life.

From then on, Benjamin's life did change. It took on a whole new dimension of giving and loving people. A happy smile greeted people who admired and inquired about his wooden carvings. Many bought gifts, some only admired Benjamin's fine workmanship but all were impressed with the loving personality Benjamin radiated.

Carving had been a talent Benjamin had enjoyed all his life. His one and a half inch steel blade with its bone handle had, under his expert guidance, changed many a scrap of wood into a soft lamb, a peaceful dove, or some other object of interest.

Everyone seemed to know about Benjamin who carved wooden animals and sold them in the streets of Jerusalem. His fame had spread even to King Herod and one of his officials came to commission Benjamin to carve a large statue to be placed in the palace courtyard.

Benjamin accepted this challenge, the greatest in his carving experience. It was to be a statue of his brother Lancus which would stand in King Herod's palace courtyard as a memorial of his brother's valor.

Weeks and weeks went by as he worked. Every minute of his days and many hours of his nights were thrown into the figure emerging from the olive wood.

Every detail of the impressive uniform had to be exact, its utility obvious yet its glamour unobscured. The head of the statue was erect, the face intelligent.

Benjamin longed to let the face of his brother reflect the gentle kindness it had shown after the death of their parents when Lancus was the one Benjamin had looked to for all his needs. Benjamin meditated as he paused in his work. It was then he realized that Lancus would not be the soldier the king knew, admired, and now wanted to honor. He took up his carving knife again. The face of his brother must now show his haughty bearing, his cold determination to serve and his complete obedience and dedication to King Herod which had gained for him the honor of commanding the king's army. The statue's face must be the true reflection of his soul.

At last the statue was completed. Standing with one hand holding his mighty sword, his shield at his side, his face showing obedience to his king, the statue of Lancus was ready to be taken to the courtyard.

Benjamin looked once more at the statue. The little lines about the eyes showed Lancus looking far into the future. Benjamin hoped that Lancus could see the Eternal King to whom his obedience and service would now be given.

In the palace courtyard the statue stood draped with a rich scarlet cover. People from miles around had come for the unveiling. The king stood up and his voice brought a stillness to the crowd.

"My fellow citizens of Jerusalem and all Judea, I welcome you here today to honor one of the greatest commanders that Judea has ever known. Lancus will ever be known for his bravery among his associates. Let the veil be drawn."

Benjamin's masterpiece was in full view of the people. They marveled and applauded the work and the dedication that had gone into this memorial statue.

Obeying a signal from King Herod, Benjamin stood up and acknowleded the plaudits produced by his masterpiece which was a symbol of desire and dedication behind King Herod's army.

s Benjamin sold his carvings by the road-side he heard rumors that wise men from the East were on their way to Bethlehem in search of a new born king. They wanted to worship him and were taking gifts to him. Benjamin thought, "If this is true, what gift can I give?"

These stories told by travelers and townsmen caused Benjamin deep thought. During his childhood, he had heard his father tell of a king to be born, a king so great that he would save the people. Often during his boyhood days he recalled his father's words. Many times as he sorrowed over his lonely and unhappy life, he wondered if this great King could help him. Could he help him break out of this prison of loneliness which his crippled condition seemed to hold him? Would this great King have some plan that could make even him, an unhappy cripple, find joy in life?

His friend Jacob and his new legs had brought new hope and joy into his life and yet, if this great King had been born, would there still not be greater happiness in his life? If this King had power to free his people, he must also know the yearnings of their hearts and how to bring peace to their souls.

Later that day as he sold his carvings he saw three strangers approaching from the direction of King Herod's palace. The camels on which they road moved with measured steps as if they seemed to feel the importance of their journey. The three strangers were elegantly dressed, their flowing robes rich in color, the jeweled trim on their head dresses flashing in the sunlight.

Excitement stirred Benjamin. The stories "were" true. These men "were" from the East. Did this mean that the rest of the story was true — that the great King, the Messiah had really been born? He watched in wonder as the travelers drew near.

The man on the camel nearest to Benjamin signaled his camel. The obedient beast of burden knelt and the stranger dismounted. To Benjamin he said, "We seek a new born babe, one called Jesus, the Christ child. Knowest thou where we can find him?"

Benjamin answered respectfully, "I do not know where he lies. Who is this child that is so important to you?"

The wise man answered, "He is the Son of God who has come to save his people. We have followed his star and will continue to follow it. We must find him."

Mounting their camels, the three wise men continued their journey. Benjamin gazed in wonderment after them.

His soul was stirred by the words of the wise man, "He is the Son of God". There was no doubt. Somehow Benjamin knew that this child was the Son of God, a knowledge that filled every part of his being. Never had he been so sure of anything before. Never had such joy filled his heart.

He must make a gift for this king to show Him that he will follow Him all the days of his life. When the Christ child grew up and gave the people his plan to free them, Benjamin would follow him, for he knew that Christ would be "the light and the way".

Yes, he would give a gift—but what? He had no money for an expensive gift from the shops in Jerusalem. Carving was his only talent. He thought of the little lambs and of the baby doves and their soft cooing just outside his window. Then an inspiration came to him. A warm burning swelled within his heart. This was his answer.

Quickly gathering up his carvings, he started for home. On his way he stopped at the home of Jacob and asked him for a ride to Bethlehem the next afternoon. The gift already existed in his mind. By the next day, his hands would bring it forth.

As Jacob looked at the courageous boy who had first made his way on stumps and now on wooden legs, his heart was stirred with love and compassion for him.

"Yes," he said, "I'll come by with the cart for you. I'd like to go to Bethlehem too. They say a child has been born there who will someday be a king. He will save his people. We'll go together, Benjamin."

Benjamin hurried on, anxious to bring to life the inspiration for his gift. Through the rest of the day and far into the night, Benjamin sat at his workbench carefully shaping and fitting together the parts of his gift. Never had any handiwork, not even the statue of Lancus, inspired him with such a feeling of joy and urgency to complete.

Warmth and happiness filled his heart as he anticipated taking his gift to the new born king. Now and then he worried, would his gift be worthy of this Messiah who was to save his people? Would his parents want or need it or think it worthy of their little son? In spite of doubts, he worked on, at times joyous with anticipation, at other times worried.

Finally he rested briefly on his bed. He was weary from the long hours of sitting at his workbench. Sleep did not come to him but his hands relaxed and his shoulders straightened from their long hours of strain over this work which meant so much to him.

Soon he was back placing the finishing touches on his gift. His tired hands rested gently on it. Then he prayed that his gift would be acceptable and worthy of the Christ child.

It was late afternoon when Benjamin heard the rumbling approach of the cart. Through his window, he saw his faithful friend Jacob pull on the reins to stop the two plodding donkeys.

Benjamin had carefully prepared himself for the journey. He was clean and well groomed. His tunic and other garments were clean but showed much wear. Covering his gift with a cloth, Benjamin made his way out the door to Jacob. He handed the covered gift to him, then pulled himself up into the wagon. Jacob did not ask about the gift. He knew Benjamin would tell him when he was ready.

Jacob lifted the reins and the donkeys moved forward to begin the five mile journey to Bethlehem. The road was rough with small holes becoming larger as they traveled from Jerusalem to Bethlehem.

When Jerusalem was left behind, Benjamin uncovered his gift. Jacob gave a little gasp of surprise.

"Benjamin, it is the most beautiful gift I have ever seen."

"Do you think it is a worthy gift to one who is to be the Messiah, the one who will save his people? I am so nervous. Sometimes I have doubts," said Benjamin.

Wise old Jacob spoke from years of experience. "There's no reason to be nervous. Everyone is afraid of the unknown. It looks as though you have worked long and hard to finish your gift." Jacob's praise comforted Benjamin. "Now is the time," continued Jacob, "to rejoice that you have finished your beautiful gift. I'm sure Joseph and Mary will welcome you and they will love your gift which honors their son."

"Do you think there could be another gift like mine?" asked Benjamin.

"Even if there is, is it not in the giving that we find true happiness in life?"

Benjamin was thoughtful. He leaned back and looked over the desert land. The sun's rays became a piercing red as they sank nearer to the horizon.

Night had come before they arrived in Bethlehem. Stars shone in the sky and the one great star which the wise men from the East had called "His star" shone more brilliantly than any other. Benjamin gazed heavenward with wonder as they rode along. The lighted sky was more beautiful than he had ever seen it. His heart was filled with adoration for this child King whose birth had been thus proclaimed.

As they traveled along, travelers said that shepherds watching their flocks had heard angels singing. Benjamin's heart almost cried with joy.

When Jacob brought the cart to a stop in front of a simple stable, Benjamin could hardly breathe because of the excitement and wonder of being there with his gift. Jacob helped him down from the wagon, then led the donkeys around so they would be out of sight.

Benjamin made his way slowly to the stable doors holding his gift in front of him. The door swung open and Joseph stood before him. Seeing Benjamin, Joseph stooped and lifted him up into his arms and set him down on the hay beside Mary and the baby. Never had Benjamin looked into eyes more beautiful, more luminous, or more radiant with love. He looked with love at Mary, then held out his gift.

Mary lifted her new born son and laid him in a wooden cradle which Benjamin had carved from his wooden legs. Tears fell on its edges as he looked upon the Son of God, the Savior of the world. He knew his gift had been accepted.

Joseph came closer to his family.

Benjamin looked up through blurred eyes as tears continued to fall. He knew at last the full meaning of Jacob's words when he said, "Thinking of others and working for their happiness is the way we find true happiness."

The keen eye of Joseph, the carpenter of Nazareth, looked upon the curved lines of the cradle and the beautiful carvings which adorned the head and the foot of the cradle. He saw the expert joining of the wood that now held the infant child. He could see where the wood for the cradle had come from.

His throat was tight with compassion and love for Benjamin who had given his all as a gift for the Christ Child. His thoughts raced on and his heart was touched, for he knew he could make some fine wooden legs for Benjamin.